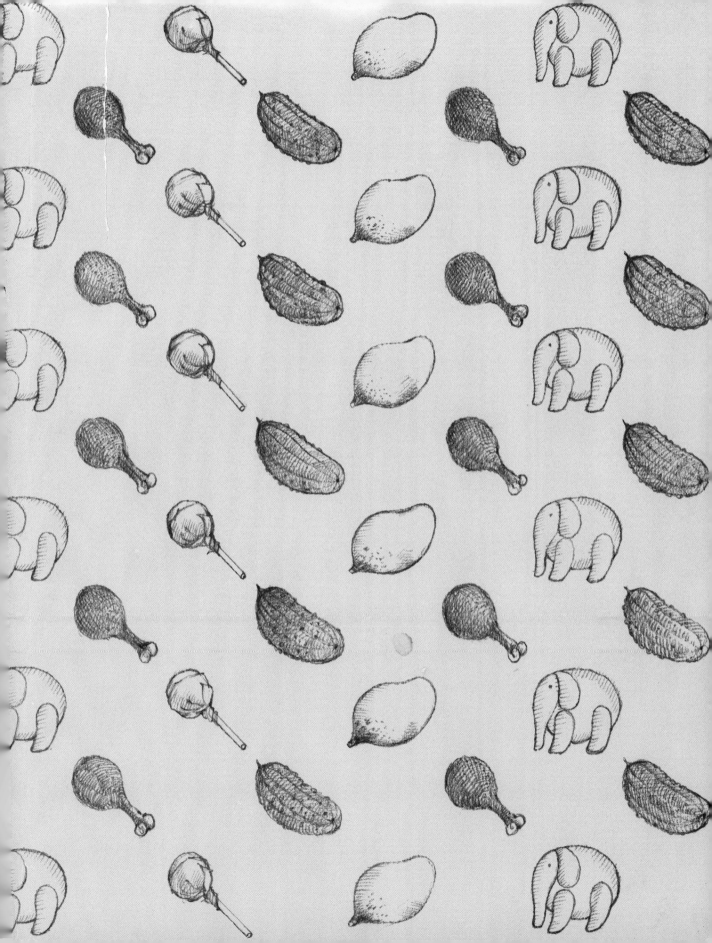

THE MANGO TOOTH

by
CHARLOTTE POMERANTZ

pictures by
MARYLIN HAFNER

GREENWILLOW BOOKS
A Division of William Morrow & Company, Inc. • New York

Library of Congress Cataloging in Publication Data
Pomerantz, Charlotte. The mango tooth.
Summary: Posy loses four teeth — and profits from each loss.
[1. Teeth—Fiction] I. Hafner, Marylin. II. Title. PZ7. P77Man
[E] 76-22664 ISBN 0-688-80070-X ISBN 0-688-84070-1 lib. bdg.

FOR JUDY AND AL

The first tooth was a mango tooth.

Posy sat on the front stoop,

eating a sweet juicy mango.

Suddenly—ouch—she bit the pit.

She licked the sore spot with her tongue.

Then she felt it with her finger.

"Mommy," she said, "my tooth is loose."

Soon afterward the tooth fell out.

She held it carefully
in the palm of her hand.
"Look, mommy, my mango tooth."
"My," said her mother.
"It's as tiny as a grain of rice."

Oh, the very first tooth was a mango tooth,
'Cause she bit the pit
And that's the truth.
In the morning time, you'll find a dime,
A dime beneath the pillow for the mango tooth.

"A dime," said Posy.

"That's two nickels.

That's ten pennies. Wow!"

Posy smiled.

"Oh, Po," said her mother.

"You look so nice without a tooth."

The number two tooth was a chicken bone tooth.
Posy sat at a long table in the lunchroom of
Public School 11, chewing on a chicken leg.
Suddenly—eeee—she bit the bone.

She poked her friend Jenny.

"Look, Jenny. My tooth came out."

"Boy, are you lucky," said Jenny.

"I know," said Posy. "I'm going to call it
my chicken bone tooth."

Oh, the number two tooth was a chicken bone tooth,

A P. S. 11 chicken bone tooth.

She bit the bone

And that's the truth.

In the morning time, you'll find a dime,

A dime beneath the pillow for the chicken bone tooth.

"Now I have two dimes," said Posy.

"That's four nickels.

That's twenty pennies. Wow!"

Posy smiled.

"Oh, Po," said her mother.

"You look so nice without two teeth."

The number three tooth was a pickle tooth.
Posy came running into her mother's study.
"Another tooth just fell out," she said.
"How did it happen?" said her mother.
Posy giggled. "I bit into a pickle," she said.
"Let me see the tooth," said her mother.
Posy opened her palm. And there it was—
as tiny as a grain of rice.
Posy laughed. "It's not a real tooth," she said.
"It's a grain of rice.
Did I fool you?"

"You little goose," said her mother.

"You don't get a dime for this one."

"How about a nickel?" said Posy.

"A nickel for a pickle."

"Not one penny," said her mother.

"All right," said Posy. "But I'll give it
a name anyway. I'll call it
my squooshy pickle tooth."

Oh, the number three tooth was a squooshy pickle tooth.
A who? A what? A squooshy pickle tooth!
Well, ha, ha, ha—that's not the truth.
In the morning time, you'll find no dime,
No dime beneath the pillow for the squooshy pickle tooth.

"No dime," said Posy.
"No two nickels.
No ten pennies.
No nothing.
Aw."

And the *real* third tooth?

Posy isn't sure.

It happened on Halloween.

"Let's dress up as witches," said Posy to Jenny.

"Do witches wear lipstick and nail polish?" asked Jenny.

"Beautiful witches do," said Posy.

So Posy and Jenny dressed up as beautiful witches,

and they carried brown paper bags and brooms.

They began on the top floor of the small apartment
house where they lived. They knocked on every door,
and when someone opened the door,
they yelled Trick or Treat!

They got seventeen pennies and one nickel.
They also got lots and lots of candy,
which they kept on eating
as they went from door to door.

It wasn't until they got home that Posy noticed
that her tooth was loose enough to pull out.
She held it up to show Jenny.
"I bet the tootsie pop did it," said Jenny.
"Or the Turkish toffy," said Posy.
"I ate two of each on the way down."

Oh, the real third tooth was a tootsie pop tooth,

Or perhaps it was a Turkish toffy tooth.

(She's not quite sure—and that's the truth.)

In the morning time, you'll find a dime,

A dime beneath the pillow for the Turkish tootsie tooth.

"Now I have three dimes," said Posy.

"That's six nickels.

 That's thirty pennies. Wow!"

 Posy smiled.

"Oh, Po," said her mother.

"You look so nice without three teeth."

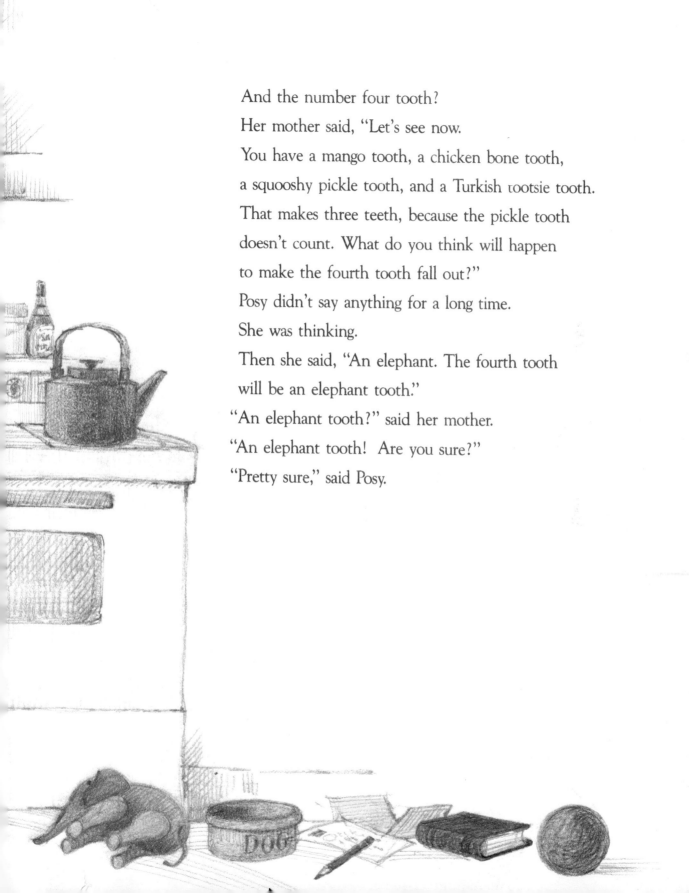

And the number four tooth?

Her mother said, "Let's see now.

You have a mango tooth, a chicken bone tooth,

a squooshy pickle tooth, and a Turkish tootsie tooth.

That makes three teeth, because the pickle tooth

doesn't count. What do you think will happen

to make the fourth tooth fall out?"

Posy didn't say anything for a long time.

She was thinking.

Then she said, "An elephant. The fourth tooth

will be an elephant tooth."

"An elephant tooth?" said her mother.

"An elephant tooth! Are you sure?"

"Pretty sure," said Posy.

"Well," said her mother, "if the fourth tooth
is an elephant tooth, you'll find *two* dimes
beneath the pillow."
"Two dimes for one tooth?" said Posy.
"Two dimes for an *elephant* tooth,"
said her mother.
Posy smiled.
"Two dimes," she said. "Wow."

A few weeks later, Posy went to Jenny's birthday party.
Everyone got a toy wristwatch, a toot whistle
and a box of cookies.

When Posy's mother came to take her home,
she said to Jenny's father,
"What a lovely party. Everybody is so busy."
"Your Posy is the busiest of all," said Jenny's father.
"She seems to have something to say to everybody."
"Posy," called her mother. "Time to go home."
"Wait," said Posy. "I just have to speak
to one more person."

When they got home, Posy opened her box
of cookies and began to eat.
"Didn't you have enough to eat at the party?"
"No," said Posy, as she took another cookie.
And another.
"What did you eat?" asked her mother.
Posy shrugged. "Just two hamburgers,
potato salad, chocolate milk, birthday cake,
ice cream—and that's all."
She popped another cookie into her mouth.

"Posy," said her mother. "You've had
  quite enough cookies."
"Just one more," said Posy. She bit down hard,
  gave a yank with her fingers—and out it came!
"My tooth fell out," said Posy.
"And it's an elephant tooth!"

"Really?" said her mother.

"Did you bump into an elephant?"

"No," said Posy. "I *bit* into an elephant."

She emptied the box of cookies onto the kitchen table.

They were animal crackers.

"Oh," said her mother. "Animal crackers.

And they are all elephants!"

"I know," said Posy. "We each got a box and

I traded animals with everybody. That's how

I got a whole boxful of just elephants."

"So that's why you were so busy talking to everyone
at the party," said her mother.
"Uh huh," said Posy, feeling the new space
with her tongue.
"How many elephants did it take?" asked her mother.
"Eleven," said Posy.

Her mother laughed. "You are right, Posy," she said.
"The number four tooth is an elephant tooth."
"That's two dimes," said Posy. "Remember?"

Oh, the number four tooth was an elephant tooth.
An elephant tooth! Is that the truth?
She ate eleven elephants—that's the truth.
For an elephant tooth, you'll find two dimes,
Two dimes beneath the pillow for the elephant tooth.

"Two dimes," said Posy.

"And I already have three dimes.

That's five dimes.

That's ten nickels.

That's fifty pennies.

That's half a dollar. Wow!"

Posy smiled. A great big smile, with
two teeth missing on the bottom,
and two teeth missing on the top.
"Oh, Po," said her mother.
"You look so nice without four teeth."

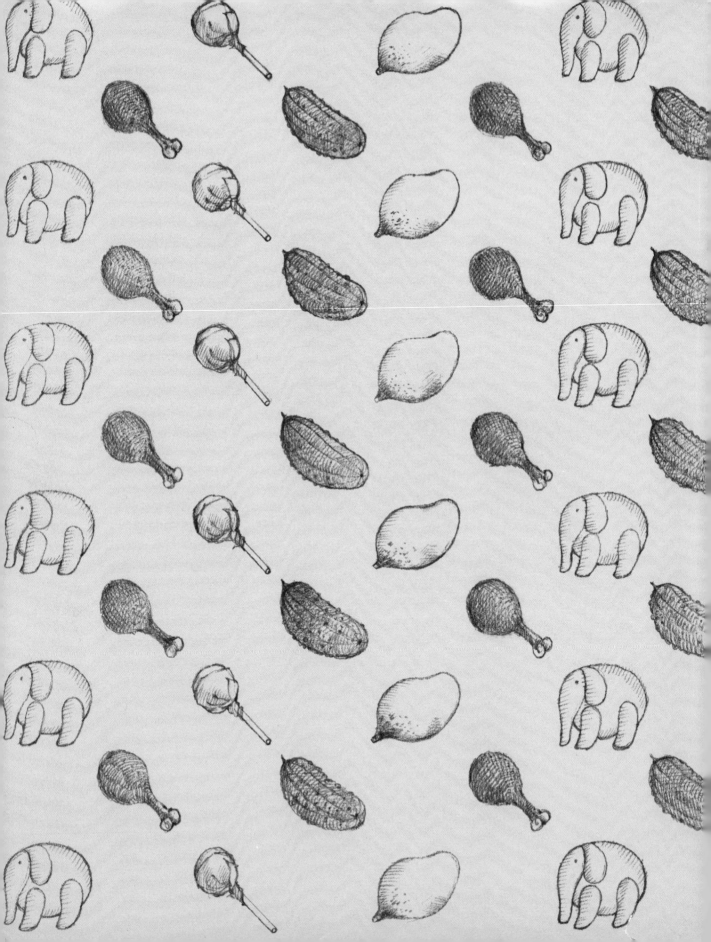

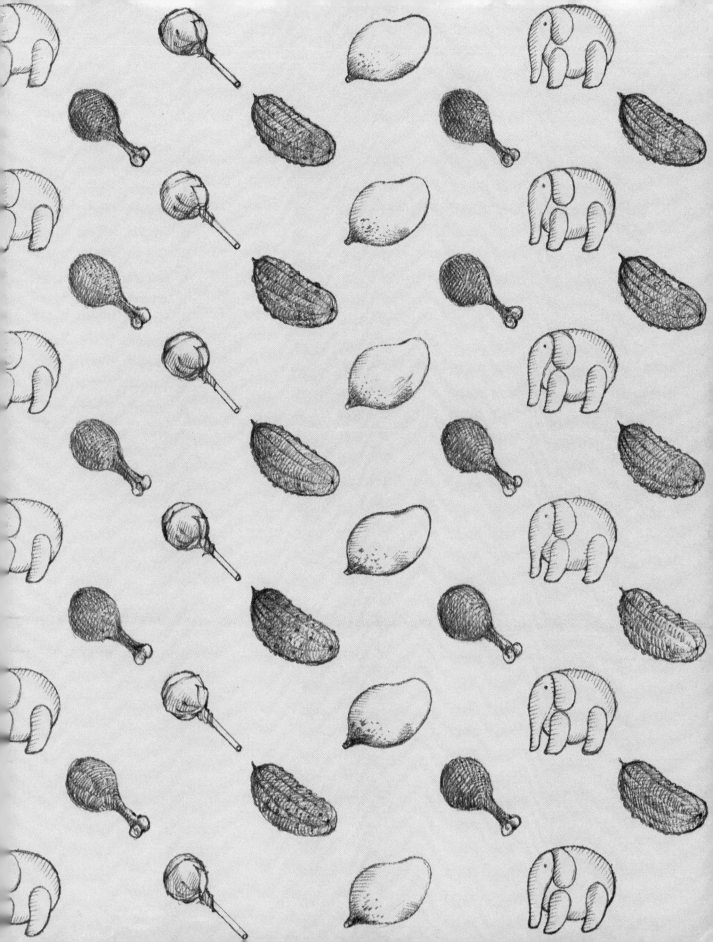

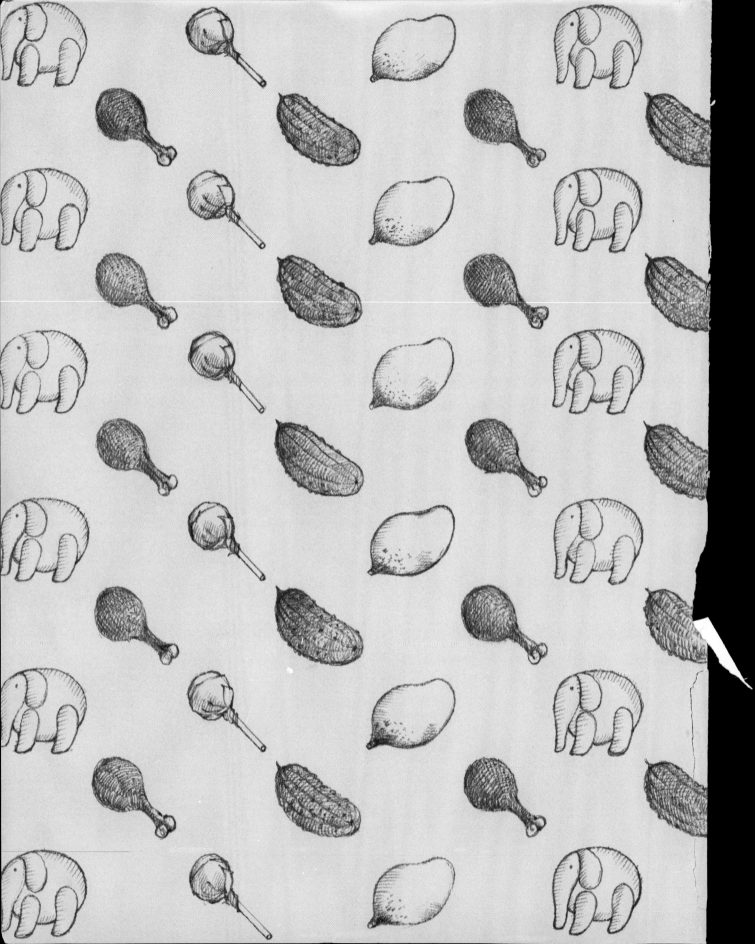